For my dad y mi abuelo.
You will always live on.
In this book y en nuestra familia.
LS

For my big crazy familia.
ZGH

Text copyright © 2021 by Laurenne Sala
Illustrations copyright © 2021 by Zara González Hoang

First edition 2021

Library of Congress Catalog Card Number pending
ISBN 978-1-5362-0943-3

21 22 23 24 25 26 CCP 10 9 8 7 6 5 4 3 2 1

Printed in Shenzhen, Guangdong, China

This book was typeset in Amasis MT Pro.
The illustrations were done in watercolor, colored pencil, and a little bit of digital magic.

Candlewick Press
99 Dover Street
Somerville, Massachusetts 02144

www.candlewick.com

Mi Casa Is My Home

WORDS BY
LAURENNE SALA

PICTURES BY
ZARA GONZÁLEZ HOANG

CANDLEWICK PRESS

¡Hi! Soy Lucía. Bienvenidos a mi casa. I live here with my big, loud, beautiful familia. I'm going to show you around.

Esta es la puerta . . . It's where Abuela likes to stand and wave to the neighbors. It's where the mail carrier leaves packages from mis tías en Puerto Rico o mi familia en España filled with turrones or dulces or gifts for our cumples.

It's a magic puerta because every time I open it, someone always
comes in. Mis primos. Los primos de mis primos. Most times,
it's Tío Jaime or Señora Veracruz from across the way.

Esta es la sala . . . It's where I build the best forts.

With big fat pillows and soft blankets to keep out the light . . .

and the hermanos.

It's where I put my feet by other feet and
snuggle up to a película con las tías.

It's where I beat Papi at cards and find toys
in the cushions and fall asleep in a pile.

Esta es la cocina . . . It's where I watch Mamá perform milagros. She takes empty pots and turns them into soups and arroces and on weekends . . . ropa vieja.

It's where everyone gathers on holidays to help and talk and ooh and aah for Abuelo as he makes his masterpiece: pavo a la española (y berenjenas para mis tíos vegetarianos).

It's where we sit at the table and pour leche condensada on tortitas and try olives and sneak bites to our dog, Capitán.

Este es el patio . . . It's where the trees remember me. They hold me when I'm lazy or help launch me up and away when I become SUPER LU!

It's where we all eat sandía

and play tag

and dominos

and Hula-Hoops with even more primos de mis primos' primos.

It's where we put on magic shows

and pretend we are ballerina pirates or chefs at a fancy restaurant.

It's where I turn the music muy muy
alta para bailar y bailar y bailar.

Este es el baño . . . It's where I shave my barba con Abuelo

and where Abuela says, "Sana sana colita de rana!"
whenever I get a cut on my knee (which happens a lot!).

Este es el cuarto de mis hermanos . . . It's where they tell me to keep out but then let me in. Me necesitan. Who else would help decide which planet is prettiest or who gets to be Tyrannosaurus rex?

It's where we meet after fights and one of us says "lo siento."
Most of the time. It's where I sneak sometimes in the dark
when I need un abrazo extra. And on Saturday mornings
because brothers make the best almohadas.

Y ESTA es mi habitación!

It's where I know I got taller when my hiding spots get smaller. Where I teach classes to my peluches at night and hang my most colorful obras de arte.

It's where Abuela puts smelly stuff on my chest
when I'm sick and Papi reads me cuentos.

Where I get tucked in con todos mis mejores amigos. It's where the lights get low and my eyelids close. Until I'm ready to wake up again tomorrow.

En mi casa. With my favorite people.

FAMILIA
AMOR
SALUD